A Glass Slipper
for Rosie

The BALLET SLIPPERS™ series

BALLET SLIPPERS™ 5

A Glass Slipper for Rosie

by Patricia Reilly Giff

illustrated by Julie Durrell

VIKING

I wish to thank Miss Susan of Dance with
Susan in Fairfield, Connecticut.

VIKING
Published by the Penguin Group
Penguin Putnam Inc., 375 Hudson Street, New York, New York 10014, U.S.A.
Penguin Books Ltd, 27 Wrights Lane, London W8 5TZ, England
Penguin Books Australia Ltd, Ringwood, Victoria, Australia
Penguin Books Canada Ltd, 10 Alcorn Avenue, Toronto, Ontario, Canada M4V 3B2
Penguin Books (N.Z.) Ltd, 182-190 Wairau Road, Auckland 10, New Zealand

Penguin Books Ltd, Registered Offices: Harmondsworth, Middlesex, England

First published in 1997 by Viking, a member of Penguin Putnam Inc.

1 3 5 7 9 10 8 6 4 2

Text copyright © Patricia Reilley Giff, 1997
Illustrations copyright © Penguin Putnam Inc., 1997

LIBRARY OF CONGRESS CATALOGING-IN-PUBLICATION DATA
Giff, Patricia Reilly.
A glass slipper for Rosie / by Patricia Reilly Giff ; illustrated by Julie Durrell.
p. cm. — (Ballet slippers ; 5)
Summary: Rosie pl... ... her grandfather on his birthday
by getting h... ...is favorite ballet.

[1. Balle... ...ays—fiction.]
I. Durrell, Julie... ... Ballet slippers ; 5.
PZ7... ...P AC

Set in OptiBrite

For Caitlin Patricia Giff,
our beautiful Caitie

Chapter 1

A skillion leaves were on the ground. A skillion more were drifting down. I swung my ballet slippers and *bourréed* down the street ahead of my best friend, Murphy. We were headed for the library.

"Don't talk," I told him. "Don't say a word. I'm trying to think."

Grandpa's birthday was coming in a few weeks. And Grandpa was my absolute favorite person. I had to dream up a perfect present. And all for one dollar and thirty-eight cents.

I began to sing. I think better that way. I sang under my breath. I knew I sounded like a crow.

Murphy knew it, too.

"You don't have to laugh like a hyena," I said. "I never said I was a rock star."

Murphy yanked up his socks. "You look like a stork, Rosie, up on one leg."

I didn't have time to say a word.

Robert Ray, that nerd, was racing up in back of us. I could hear him calling. I could hear him breathing. "Wait up, you guys," he said. It sounded as if he had a cold.

Robert always sounded that way. He talked through his nose.

"Enemy in sight," Murphy said.

I was about to speed up, but the library was right in front of us. We turned in, with Robert sliding up the railing behind us, if you can picture that. He was honking like a goose.

Murphy headed for the science section. He

was trying to find out something about the fat black ants in his yard. Murphy loved stuff like that.

I went straight to the ballet books.

Robert stood at the entrance for a minute, trying to decide. Then he went after Murph, snorting all the way.

"Whew," I said under my breath. I had no time for Robert, no time for anything. I had to find a ballet, the most wonderful, the most stupendous ballet. And I had to do it in about three-and-a-half minutes.

Ballet lessons began at 4:00 o'clock, and finding a ballet had been last week's homework.

I crouched down on the floor. All the dance books were on the bottom shelf. We had done *The Nutcracker.* We had done *Sleeping Beauty.* We had even done *Swan Lake.* The rest of the kids had checked out everything else. No, wait a minute.

A blue book with *Cinderella* on the cover.

I sat back on my ankles with the book in my hand. Yes, wonderful. Terrific.

It was Grandpa's favorite ballet. My grandmother Genevieve had danced *Cinderella*. Grandpa had been in the audience. He had fallen in love with her on the spot. The next day he had bought her a tiny glass slipper on a chain. It was there still, in his bedroom drawer.

I had told Murphy all about it. "Yucks," was all he had said.

And he was going to say yucks again. I had forgotten my library card. I shook my head. I had promised I wouldn't borrow his anymore.

Last time I had used a chocolate mint to keep my place in *Children of Switzerland*. It had melted into a chocolate mountain. And Murphy and I had been in big trouble with the librarian for days.

I looked up at the clock. I was late. Very late. Murphy was nowhere in sight. But Robert Ray

was honking his way over to me.

"Hey Robert," I asked. "How about lending me your library card?"

He reached into his pocket. One thing you had to say about Robert. He was generous. One thing you had to say about his library card. It was filthy.

I took it with two fingers. . . . So did Ms. Berry. "You're supposed to use your own card, Rosie O'Meara," she said.

I opened my mouth. "This is the last time." I crossed my fingers, just in case. Then I handed Robert his card. I tucked *Cinderella* and my ballet slippers under one arm and headed for Scranton Avenue and the Dance with Miss Deirdre studio.

While I shuffled through the leaves along the curb, it hit me. A terrific idea. Grandpa's birthday. *Cinderella* would be his birthday surprise.

Robert Ray was hollering. "Wait up, Rosie."

6

That kid was always around when you didn't need him.

I didn't wait. Instead I waved over my shoulder with three fingers, and turned the corner.

Chapter 2

I wanted to get my *Cinderella* idea in first. I kept raising my hand, but Miss Deirdre acted as if she didn't even see me.

"*Entrechat quatre,*" said Miss Deirdre. "First do a *demi-plié*. Spring into the air . . ." She frowned. "Rosie? Are you listening?"

"Spring into the air." I pulled down my hand.

"Then quickly swap the position of your legs," said Miss Deirdre, "front to back. . . ." She made a cross with her fingers, first one in front, then the other.

I thought she was finished with *entrechats* at last. I raised my hand again.

"And then back again," Miss Deirdre said, "A famous Russian dancer, Nijinsky, could cross his feet six times."

I was getting tired of waving my arm around. We were probably going to be talking about *entrechats* all afternoon.

Miss Serena played a thump on the piano. Everyone sprang up, ready to try an *entrechat*.

I sprang, too. I kept my eye on Karen. She always knew what we were supposed to be doing.

Karen had begun a *demi-plié*, but Stephanie stretched one leg out in front of her.

Stephanie was smiling as if she knew what she was doing, so I stuck a leg out.

Wrong. Miss Deirdre was frowning. I stuck

my leg back in. Karen was up in the air now. She did a quick crisscross forward and back with her feet, and made a perfect landing.

"Did you forget . . ." I began, but Miss Deirdre was talking louder than I was.

"Yes, lovely," she was telling Karen.

I jumped. No good. I landed before I could change feet back again.

Miss Deirdre came over to me. "Think of your feet, your legs." She stretched out each word like bubble gum. *"Understand what's going on."*

I sprang and landed forty times and never got it right.

I was sick of the whole thing. We were never going to get to *Cinderella.*

"Did you forget—" I began again.

Miss Deirdre clapped her hands. That meant another switch. First we were clouds floating through the blue sky. Then we were horses galloping...

... near the hall door. I had to go to the bathroom. Miss Deirdre would have an absolute fit if she saw me.

I galloped to the door when her back was turned. I charged down the hall and into the ladies' room.

Miss Deirdre had the prettiest ladies' room in the world. She and Miss Serena had painted Clara from *The Nutcracker* on one wall, and Romeo and Juliet on another. The Sleeping Beauty was asleep on the ceiling.

I took a peek at my face in the mirror, thinking about Cinderella.

Did I look like Cinderella? Did I look like the Fairy Godmother? I made a horrible face in the mirror. Did I look like a wicked stepsister?

I slid down the hall again, ready to be a horse or a cloud. But cloud time was over. I tiptoed across the floor.

It was finally idea time. In the two minutes since I had gone, everyone had sat down in a circle on the floor. Everyone was talking at the same time.

And everyone had a different idea. Stephanie wanted to do *The Nutcracker* all over again. This time she thought she was going to be Clara, the star, I guess.

But Miss Deirdre shook her head at every single idea.

"Too hard," she said about one. "Too long," she said about another.

All this time, I was waving my hand in the air. You could have seen me a mile away and I was saying, *"Cinderella . . . Cinderella."*

At last Miss Deirdre looked in my direction. So did everyone else. No one said a word for a moment.

Miss Deirdre smiled and nodded slowly.

Miss Serena played a few thumps on the piano.

Everybody began to clap.

"I'm dying to be Cinderella," Stephanie said.

"I'm dying more than you are," said Karen. "It's my turn to be the star."

"It was my idea," I said.

Miss Deirdre held up one hand. We all knew what that meant. "Being the star is not the most important thing. . . ." she began.

"Right." I knew what was coming next.

Miss Deirdre made a circle with pointy pink fingernails. "It's the ballet that matters."

"Right," I said again.

Karen and Stephanie both made faces at me. But this time I didn't care about being the star. It really was the ballet that mattered.

I was so happy that we were going to surprise Grandpa. I knew he'd love this. I knew this was the best birthday present I could give him.

On the way home, I stopped at the Crow's Nest Country Store for a gumball. I could feel the syrup of happiness in my chest.

Robert Ray was running his dirty fingers

through the whole gumball barrel. "Gross," I
told him.

"I'm looking for a purple one," he said.
"Want one?"

"They don't come in purple." I grabbed two
reds off the top, left my money on the tray, and
waved to Mr. Mooney behind the counter. I
started for home thinking of Grandpa. How
would I ever keep the surprise a secret?

Chapter 3

I came up the path watching my little brother, Andrew. He was crawling around in the bushes. He had been in there for days, digging for treasure.

Grandpa poked his head out the window. "Andrew, my boy," he said, "you've got holes so deep the bushes are going to fall over."

"I know it," said Andrew. "And maybe the house, too."

Grandpa saw me and waved. "Stew for dinner, Rosie," he called. "Thick as a London fog . . ."

". . . with great slabs of carrots," I finished for him.

I hated Grandpa's stew. I wouldn't let him know that in a million years, though. Instead, on stew nights, I pushed the food around on my plate. I played checkers with the carrots. I fed the meat to Jake, our cat.

I stopped at the steps now, looking at Andrew. He was filthy, dirt on his shirt, mud on his jeans, and . . .

"What's that on your face?" I asked.

Andrew's nose was purple. So were his cheeks and chin. "Don't be afraid," he said. "It's me with paint. Purple for a pirate mask."

Grandpa winked at me. He pulled his head back in and shut the window.

"Grandpa's got a secret," Andrew said.

"What . . . ?" I began, doing a little *jeté* up the steps.

"Maybe it's a surprise for you." Andrew sat back on his heels. "Is your birthday coming?"

I shook my head. "Not for a long time."

I looked down at the holes around the bushes. A few gray roots were sticking up. "Did Mother see the mess you're making?"

Andrew shook his head. "Don't worry, Rosie. I'm going to be rich when I find the treasure. I'll share all my money with you and Mommy and Daddy."

He stopped for a breath. "And I'll give Grandpa something special, something really special."

I put my hand on Andrew's head. I could feel the heat of the sun, and gritty bits from the dirt he was digging. "You're a nice boy," I told him.

But Andrew was busy again. He grabbed two tablespoons and dug with both hands at once.

At the same time he was singing, "I have a new friend. His name is Raymond, I think."

"Nice," I said, and went into the house.

My mother was sitting at the table with my father. Her shoes were off. She had peachy polish on her toenails. Her feet looked absolutely terrific.

They were talking with Grandpa about something. I heard my mother say, "Do it, Pa. It's sad for us, but wonderful for you."

"What's wonderful?" I asked.

They looked at each other. "What smells wonderful is my stew," Grandpa said. "I've put in some celery this time."

My mother wiggled her toes. "I am so glad to have my shoes off. I was on my feet every minute at work."

She smiled at me. "Tell us about the ballet lessons."

I sighed. I knew she wasn't going to tell me whatever it was. I'd have to find out for myself.

"We're learning *entrechat quatre*." The word sounded neat on my tongue. It was French, I knew.

I looked at my mother. She had on one silver earring that shimmered in the light.

"Where's . . ." I began.

She touched her other ear. "Another earring lost? I can't believe it."

I tried an *entrechat* for them. It didn't work.

"Don't worry," Grandpa said. "You'll figure it out. You have to think about each part."

Andrew stamped into the kitchen. "This treasure is deep down," he said.

At the stove, Grandpa nodded. "I remember Genevieve doing *entrechats*. Straight up, her feet crossing and crossing again."

I thought about Genevieve, my grandmother, who had carried the little glass slipper around for luck. She had been a famous ballerina. I wished I had known her.

Then I looked out the window. I could see Amy Stetson next door.

Amy was a ballerina, too. She exercised a hundred times a day, a million times a day.

And that was absolutely what I was going to do. I was going to be a wonderful ballerina who knew how to do *entrechats*. And I was going to surprise Grandpa with *Cinderella*.

I even ate a tiny piece of stew meat, and one carrot.

I forgot to find out what my mother was telling Grandpa to do.

Chapter 4

I was sitting on the studio floor. "Do you remember what *choreography* means?" Miss Deirdre asked.

"It's making up the dances," Karen said.

"Wonderful," said Miss Deirdre.

"That's what I was going to say," said Stephanie.

Sure.

"You know the story of *Cinderella*," Miss Deirdre said. "Now we have to show it as a story in dance."

Murphy was peeking in the window. He was squishing up his nose to make me laugh.

I tried a wrinkle-the-nose-and-stick-out-the-tongue face back at him.

Miss Deirdre raised her eyebrows at me. "Are you the wicked stepsister?" she asked.

Everyone laughed. That Murphy.

Miss Deirdre pointed to Maureen. "Cinderella." To Stephanie. "The fairy god-mother."

I sat up straight. "Julie," said Miss Deirdre, "you'll be the stepmother, and . . . "

What was left?

"Two stepsisters," Miss Deirdre said. "Karen and Rosie." She smiled. "We know you make great faces, Rosie."

Thank you, Murphy, I said to myself. But Karen and I were smiling at each other. It would be neat to be stepsisters.

Miss Deirdre had us up, all of us fooling

around with different steps: *jetés, bourées, pliés.* I tried a couple of faces.

Murphy thought I was making them at him.

It was fun; it was wonderful. I could see how it was going to be.

Karen and I *bouréed* across the room. We pointed at Cinderella. We frowned at her. We made believe we were laughing at her.

Miss Deirdre saw our stepsister faces. "Good mime." She pointed at Karen. "You're Gouda." She pointed at me. "You're Gorgonzola."

"Those are the names of cheeses," Karen said. She rolled her eyes at me.

"Right," said Miss Deirdre. "Good joke, isn't it?"

Now we were laughing at ourselves. Two pieces of cheese. The stepsisters.

I mimed another face at Murphy in the window. Too late, I saw he was gone.

Robert Ray was there instead. His nose was pressed against the window.

He looked like an undersea monster.

I mimed back the worst face I could.

A moment later, it was 5:00 o'clock. Miss Serena played a *tum-ta-dum* on the piano. That was the signal to clap for Miss Deirdre.

Then one last thing. I raised my hand. "When are we going to do this?"

Miss Deirdre looked at the calendar on her pink wall. "One month from today," she said.

I took a breath. I couldn't believe it.

"That's my Grandpa's birthday," I told her. "And *Cinderella* is his favorite ballet."

"Lovely," said Miss Deirdre. "We'll dedicate the ballet to him."

Miss Serena played some tinkling music. "Lovely," she said, too.

It was the best luck I had ever had.

Karen and I picked up our stuff. We slid out

of our ballet slippers and *bouréed* out the door.

We tiptoed around the alley. Robert Ray was still there. He was probably still making faces. He didn't even bother to notice there was no one left to make faces at.

Karen and I began to gallop. Karen was a horse person.

The whole time I was telling myself to watch out. I couldn't say one word about *Cinderella* to Grandpa.

I couldn't even think of it.

The trouble was I always told Grandpa everything. It would be so hard not to tell him this.

Karen galloped off down Scranton Avenue, and I turned in at our street.

I could see Andrew digging. Someone else was there, too.

I stopped. I couldn't believe it. What was Robert Ray doing crawling around our bushes?

He must have seen Karen and me leaving after all. Never mind galloping. He must have flown.

I went up the front path. I looked at him out of the corner of my eye.

Andrew was sitting in the dirt. He had streaks of mud on his purple face. "No treasure yet," he said. "Here's my friend Ray."

Robert Ray stuck his disgusting face out from the bushes. "Robert," he said. He held one arm over his head. I guess he was pretending to be a ballet dancer.

"Robert?" Andrew was saying, "I thought it was Ray."

"Last name," said Robert.

I made believe Robert was one of the bushes. I started around the side.

In back of me, Andrew was saying, "I told you Grandpa had a surprise, Rosie."

I stopped and looked back.

"Ask him. You'll see."

"All right." I had to smile at Andrew. His eyes looked so blue in his purple, muddy face.

"It's not a good surprise," Andrew was telling Robert. "Rosie won't like it. She'll even hate it, I think."

I opened the back door.

I thought I heard Andrew say something about Betsy Beneath. That's the little town where Genevieve, my grandmother, was born.

Everyone was in the kitchen again. My mother and father looked at each other when I came in.

"It's time to tell her, Pa," my father said.

I took a breath.

I hoped Andrew was wrong. I hoped I'd love what Grandpa had to tell me.

Chapter 5

We were having chicken for dinner. It was the white soupy kind. It had peas floating around.

It was worse than stew.

Andrew came in, we said grace, and Grandpa began to talk.

Everything sounded all right at first.

Grandpa told my favorite story of Betsy Beneath. "They say an old pirate woman is buried there," he began. "She's right beneath the crossroad."

"Betsy," I said.

Then Grandpa reminded us that Genevieve had learned ballet there. "On a tiny farm near the sea in Cornwall, England," he said.

He told us when they were first married, they had gone back. "Genevieve . . . " he began.

Andrew finished for him. ". . . danced over the radishes and the peas."

"*Jetéd* over them," I said.

Grandpa nodded, smiling.

But my mother and father weren't smiling. "Tell Rosie about your news," my father said.

Grandpa took a deep breath. "I haven't seen Betsy Beneath for . . . " He looked up at the ceiling.

I looked at my mother's face, and then at Grandpa's. Grandpa didn't want to tell me his news. I could see that.

I felt something inside my chest turn right over. *Betsy Beneath,* I said inside my head.

"How far away is—" I began.

"It's forever away," said Andrew. "You have to take a rocket plane, I think."

Grandpa shook his head. "It's not *that* far," he said.

I rounded up a couple of peas and stuck them in a row.

"Genevieve's cousin asked me to come," Grandpa said.

I nodded. "That's nice. Someday when I'm grown up, I'll go with you."

My mother was shaking her head. So was my father.

"It would be nice to see Betsy Beneath again," said Grandpa.

"Yes," said my mother. "We'll have to do without you for a month." She narrowed her eyes just a little bit at me.

I knew what she meant. *Don't be selfish. Don't be mean.* She did that all the time.

I opened my mouth. I nodded my head. "That's nice," I told Grandpa again.

Grandpa gave me the most wonderful smile. "That's my Rosie," he said. "I knew you'd want me to go."

"What about me?" Andrew asked. "I want you to go."

"Andrew," said Grandpa. "I knew I could count on you."

My mother and father were talking about what he'd bring: a warm jacket, his hat rolled up into his pocket.

I pushed two more peas into the *don't eat* row. And then I thought about *Cinderella*. I waited for them to stop talking about jackets and hats.

I could hardly say the word. "When?"

"Next week, I think," said Grandpa.

"You're going to miss your birthday?" Andrew said. "Your birthday cake with the chocolate pudding in the middle, and a thousand candles?"

Grandpa gave him a sad nod.

"And you won't be back for a month?" I asked.

"It's far," Grandpa said. "If I go, I have to . . ."

My mother was giving me that stare again.

I shoved the whole row of peas into my mouth. I took a couple of quick bites of chicken. I hardly even tasted them.

"I think I'm going outside," I said. "Murphy is probably waiting for me right this minute."

"How about homework?" my mother began.

I shook my head. "No homework." It was true. We had had a substitute teacher that day. She had forgotten all about it.

Outside, I looked around. I could see Murphy across the street. I could see Robert Ray.

What was Murphy doing with Robert Ray?

I went back into the house and slammed the door. I went straight up to my bedroom.

Over my bed was a picture of Genevieve. She was wearing feathers in her hair and a white tutu.

"Everything is spoiled," I told her.

I remembered something Grandpa had said about Genevieve. "Every time something went wrong," he said, "Genevieve would practice ballet. *Pliés* and *bourées, arabesques,* and *jetés.*"

I pushed a chair out of my way. I did an *arabesque.* And then I tried an *entrechat.*

I jumped, crossing my feet, but landed before I could cross them back again.

Chapter 6

"Ballet is a story," said Miss Deirdre. "When you dance, you're telling the person's story."

I closed my eyes. I could say the rest by heart.

"Know your person," Miss Deirdre said. "Understand her."

Karen leaned over. "Understand," she whispered. "You are a piece of cheese."

Miss Deirdre frowned. "Tell the story with your face," she was saying, "with your arms, your legs . . ."

"Tell it with your heart," Stephanie said.

"Yes," said Miss Deirdre, up on her toes.

"And with costumes," said Karen.

"Certainly," said Miss Deirdre.

I tried to get excited about costumes, but I couldn't.

Next to me, Karen was talking about step-sister costumes. "We'll have to wear two. Everyday tutus to boss Cinderella around. Then something special for the ball. Something with glitter—" she broke off. "I love glitter."

I nodded. Everyone split up to practice.

First I watched Maureen as Cinderella. She was drooping. Her head was down, her arms at her sides, her fingers limp. She was at the fire-place, sad and alone.

Joy was the prince. Her hair was stuck up with Miss Serena's bobby pins. She was scoot-ing around, close to the ground. She was trying to fit people with pretend glass slippers. It made me think of Genevieve's glass slippers.

Grandpa would have loved this whole thing.

In another corner, Stephanie was trying out an idea for the fairy godmother. She waved a wand around as she *bouréed* across the floor. She pretended to tap Cinderella on the head with it.

If someone *bouréed* toward me like an elephant, holding a wand like a sword, I'd get out of the way fast.

I couldn't even smile at that. I felt so sad about Grandpa.

And something else.

Robert Ray was at the window again. His tongue was hanging out, like Homer, Murphy's dog.

Worse than a nerd, he was a pain. He was hanging around with my little brother Andrew. He was digging for treasure. Could you believe that? A kid my age?

And he was hanging around on Murphy's steps, too. Murphy was supposed to be *my* best friend.

Someone else was going past the window now. It was Grandpa wearing red plaid pants.

Karen and I began to work on our stepsister steps. That's what Karen called them, giggling.

We were mean. We made believe we were hitting Cinderella.

We made believe we were hitting each other.

We did it all with ballet steps.

I almost forgot about feeling sad. And even Miss Deirdre smiled and clapped for us. "This is going to be wonderful," she said.

We worked a little more, and then the time was up. "Next time, we'll talk about costumes," said Miss Deirdre.

I was the last one out today. Karen galloped up ahead of me on the way to the dentist.

Stephanie *bouréed* along, still holding the wand.

I went slowly up, thinking about Grandpa's birthday. I needed a present for him now.

But what?

At the top of the stairs, I stopped. Robert Ray and Murph were bouncing a ball against Delano's Delicious Chocolates.

Mrs. Delano would have a fit listening to the clonking sound.

Robert turned with the ball. I knew he didn't mean to hit me. But I got it right in the head. I really did see stars, just the way they say on television.

It was just too much.

I sat down on the steps of Dance with Miss Deirdre. I began to cry.

Murphy's mouth was open. Murph had never seen me cry before.

And Robert Ray said "I'm sorry" forty million times.

Out of the corner of my eye, I could see
someone coming down the alley.

Long legs. Red plaid pants.

Grandpa.

I cried even more.

Chapter 7

Grandpa sat down on the edge of the steps with me. "Good thing I was getting plane tickets at the travel agency," he said. "I can walk Rosie home now."

Murphy and Robert nodded. They were both staring at me.

Grandpa reached into his pocket and pulled out a couple of quarters. "Here," he told the boys. "Enough money for two gumballs each at the Crow's Nest Country Store."

Robert put his hand out, but Murph shook

his head. Murph never likes to take money from anyone.

"I know how it is," Grandpa said. "No one likes to whack a friend on the head."

They both looked happier. They took the quarters and raced up the street. Just before they turned the corner, Murphy looked back. "See you later, O'Meara," he told me. "Soon as you feel better."

"All right," I said, sniffling a little.

"I'll get you a gumball," Murphy called. "Red. Your favorite."

Grandpa and I didn't talk for a few minutes. I still couldn't stop crying. I rubbed at the lump on my head.

What was I ever going to do without Grandpa?

"I was hit on the head once," Grandpa said. He handed me a polka-dot handkerchief. "I think I was just about your age."

I nodded.

"It was a surprise."

"Yes," I said.

"Bad surprises aren't good," Grandpa said, trying to make me laugh.

I didn't laugh, but I had to smile. I loved Grandpa's face, the laugh lines around his eyes.

"That's better," he said. "Did you have a great ballet lesson?"

I nodded. I opened my mouth, ready to tell him about *Cinderella*. Before I could say a word, Grandpa was talking.

"I remember something," he said. "That time I was hit by a ball?"

I looked up at him.

"I cried," Grandpa said. "But not because of the ball. It was something else."

"Really?" I looked away from him quickly. Mrs. Delano was coming out the back door of her shop. She waved at us.

I kept waving even after she went back inside.

"Funny," Grandpa said. "I haven't thought about that in years. I was crying because . . ." He laughed. "I can't even remember now what I was crying about."

I was about to begin with *Cinderella* again, but Grandpa took his plane ticket out of his pocket. "These are refundable," he said.

"What does that mean exactly?" I asked.

Grandpa tapped the pale blue envelope. "You can get your money back if you don't use them."

"Oh," I said.

Grandpa patted my shoulder. "I'll tell you something, Rosie. I don't know what I'd do without you and Andrew."

I could see how shiny Grandpa's eyes were. If I didn't know better, I'd think he was about to cry.

"And you, Rosie-Posie," he said, "are just like your grandmother Genevieve. Every time I see you dance, I think of her."

I thought about the picture of Genevieve over my bed, and the little glass slipper in Grandpa's drawer. And even though I still had tears in my own eyes, I could feel the syrup of happiness in my chest. "I love you, Grandpa," I said.

"Me, too," he said. He stood up. "What do you say? We'll take ourselves down to the travel place and turn in the tickets. Then we'll get ourselves some gumballs."

I couldn't believe it. "You're not going? You're not going to see Betsy Beneath and the cousins?"

"And miss my birthday here with you?" he said. "Miss my birthday cake with a hundred candles?"

"A thousand candles," I said in an Andrew voice.

"And my birthday surprises?"

I stood up. "Are you sure?" I said, giving him one last chance to change his mind.

He was grinning at me. "Sure, I'm sure," he said.

I felt as if I was going to burst. I gave the lump on my head one last rub.

Then I twirled down the alleyway, my arms over my head.

"Come on, Grandpa," I said. "Beat you to the Crow's Nest Country Store."

Chapter 8

Murphy had an idea. He was building an ant mall. And I was helping. We were using ice-pop sticks for escalators and old candy boxes for stores.

We had sprinkled stuff around for the ants to buy: sugar and chocolate bits and a crushed-up pretzel.

And they were buying. Ants were coming from everywhere.

Every two minutes, Murphy would say, "Get your ice-cold lemonade here."

We were laughing and having the best time, until Murphy started an almost-fight.

It began with Robert Ray and ended up with Grandpa.

I had spotted Robert Ray all the way down on Orient Street, but he was on his way here. I knew it.

I shaded my eyes, and watched him coming, skinny legs and . . . "Robert Ray's head is shaped like an ant's," I told Murph.

I did a quick *jeté* over the ant mall, laughing at my own joke.

Murphy didn't laugh. He started to build a parking lot with sticks from the driveway. "You're a little mean to Robert Ray," he said.

I stopped in the middle of a second *jeté* and nearly smashed the ant mall. Then I stood very still.

Murphy wasn't looking at me. His head was bent over his parking lot. I knew he was waiting for what I'd say.

"I thought you thought . . ." I began and started over. "Don't you think Robert is a nerd? A dork?"

"Yup." Murphy raised one shoulder in the air. "But . . ."

Across the street I could see the back end of Andrew. He was digging for treasure again.

"Robert Ray even plays with little kids," I said, pointing. "Robert Ray even follows me around at ballet."

Murphy looked up. "Do you know why?"

"I told you. He's a dork."

Murphy didn't say anything. He began to sprinkle sugar in his parking lot. Then he leaned over. He spit gently to wet the whole thing down.

I sat on the edge of the walk. I was careful not to get in the way of the ants. I was waiting.

It was a long wait. Robert Ray had crossed the street now.

I stretched out my legs and began to flex my

toes. *Hello, toes,* I said in my mind. I drew them closer to me.

Murphy still wasn't talking.

I hated that about Murphy. He won every contest with me. Who would blink first?

Not Murphy.

Who would swallow first?

Murphy would drown first.

And now who would talk first?

I sighed. *Good-bye, toes,* I thought. I pushed them away from me as hard as I could.

"All right," I asked Murphy. "Why?"

"Why what?" he said.

I could hear Andrew yelling. "Hey, Raymond Robert . . ."

"Why is he doing all that stuff? Playing with Andrew . . . following—"

"Hi, guys," Robert said, from the end of the path.

I didn't answer him. Instead I told Murphy, "I'm getting mad at you."

I picked an ant off my leg and sent it on its way to the parking lot. I still didn't look at Robert Ray.

After a minute, I could hear him crossing the street to Andrew.

"See?" Murphy sat back on his heels. "You did it again."

"I didn't do one thing." I scrambled to my feet. I looked across the street.

Robert Ray was looking back.

Why . . . ?

Murphy tossed a stone out of an ant's way.

For some reason, I could almost hear Miss Deirdre say, "Know your person."

I bit my cheek. I was a piece of cheese. Maureen was Cinderella. Stephanie was the fairy godmother . . .

And then it hit me. Robert Ray wanted to be friends.

That's why he was hanging around.

Good grief.

Then I sighed. Poor Robert Ray. Poor nerdy Robert Ray.

Murphy knew what I was thinking. "See," he said. He said it nicely, though.

"See yourself," I said.

We watched Grandpa coming outside. "Grandpa's not going to Betsy Beneath after all," I said, in case he hadn't heard.

Murphy said something under his breath. It sounded like "poor Grandpa."

I sat there for another minute. "He's not going because he doesn't want to miss his birthday. He doesn't want to miss his cake."

Murphy didn't say anything.

I stood up. I opened my mouth. Then I closed it again. I stepped over the ant mall and rushed across the street.

I passed Andrew and Robert Ray and slammed into the house.

Chapter 9

It was Thursday. Amy Stetson and I were in her bedroom. We had pulled every box out of the closet.

We looked at the things on the floor: tutus, feathers, tiny diamond tiaras, baby-soft slippers with laces.

Then Amy held up a pale yellow leotard that sparkled. "This will fit," she said. "And I think a stepsister might wear diamonds even at home."

She rooted around for a skirt with ribbons,

and tossed them both to me. "Let's see how they look."

I stood behind the closet door, peeled off my sweatsuit, and slid into the leotard.

The whole time I was thinking about Grandpa.

Amy was holding onto the bedpost. "It's my *barre* at home," she said.

She raised one leg up and down, her toes pointed. "I'm trying to make my muscles like rubber bands, not like sticks."

She frowned, looking over her shoulder at me. "Why do you get your hair all chopped off like that?"

"It's Albert the barber," I said. "I tell him and tell him. . . ."

Amy wasn't paying attention. She went across the room on her toes to look for something in her dresser.

Amy looked like a ballerina no matter what she did. Her head was high and her neck was long. Her back was always straight.

I loved being in Amy's room. She always told me about ballet, or gave me something from her closet, a ribbon, or a sparkly barrette, or . . .

But today was different. Today I felt terrible.

Grandpa wasn't going to Betsy Beneath because . . . I took a breath. Because he didn't want to miss his birthday. Because . . .

Because why?

"We need some goo," she said.

"What?"

"Gloop," she said, and pulled out a bottle of clear thick stuff.

"Now sit on the floor," she told me. She dumped half the bottle over my head.

I watched her in the mirror. The stuff was almost like glue. Amy slicked back my hair so I looked like Andrew.

Three minutes later she stuck a little bun on back with a thousand bobby pins.

I looked into the mirror. I couldn't believe it was me.

"A transformation," said Amy.

"What's . . ." I began. I turned my head from one side to the other. I looked like someone, but I wasn't sure who it was.

"Never mind," Amy said.

"I have to go home," I told her. "I have to show Grandpa."

"Don't you like—" Amy began.

I threw my arms around her and gave her a hug. "I love it," I said.

She reached for a bottle of perfume. She sprayed a pile of it around me.

And then I was down the stairs, my feet barely touching the floor.

Mrs. Stetson was fooling around with her plants that looked like strings. "Beautiful," she said.

Outside I stopped. I could see Murphy across the street. His mouth opened when he saw me. I waved, an I'm-not-mad-at-you wave. Then I went across the driveway.

I couldn't wait to show Grandpa. I kept thinking of Grandpa seeing me in *Cinderella*. And then I thought about Betsy Beneath again.

I stopped. Grandpa was staying home because of me.

I took a deep breath, then I opened the back door. Grandpa was doing his crossword puzzle at the kitchen table.

He stared at me for a moment, looking over the top of his glasses. "You look like Genevieve," he said, "the first time I ever saw her." He smiled. "She was a little older, of course."

I swallowed. "That's what I wanted to talk to you about," I said. "Genevieve and Betsy Beneath."

Chapter 10

I had swept the patio, but a couple of leaves were blowing across the cement now.

I didn't have time to pay attention to leaves.

I was having a birthday party for Grandpa. It was a much-too-early party.

Grandpa was going to miss *Cinderella*.

And I was going to miss Grandpa.

But the other day, I had told him, "You've got to go, Grandpa. You've got to see every single thing at Betsy Beneath."

"The old farm?" Grandpa asked, smiling.

"And the cousins," I said.

"But . . ." Grandpa had begun.

I crossed my fingers behind my back. "You'll be back in two minutes," I said.

"A month," said Grandpa.

"And you'll tell me all about it."

Grandpa had stood there, looking at me over his glasses.

I had dug my fingers into the palms of my hands. I had told myself, *If you cry, Rosie O'Meara, I'll never speak to you again.*

I had to laugh at the idea of never talking to myself again.

So Grandpa had watched my face for another second, then he nodded. "There's something I want you to have."

He went into his bedroom and came back with Genevieve's little glass slipper cupped in his hands. "I always meant it for you," he said.

I hugged Grandpa, thinking Genevieve

would be happy he was going back to see Betsy Beneath.

I went upstairs and put the slipper on my dresser. I was going to keep it there forever.

Then Grandpa and I had walked over to We'll Get You There Travel Agency and bought tickets for Betsy Beneath.

And right now, right this minute, I was getting ready for the party. I was glad it was warm enough for a picnic. I had chipped in my one dollar and thirty-eight cents, and my mother had given me the rest. We were having cake with a thousand candles, ice cream, and soda, and . . .

"Hey, Rosie," said a voice over the fence.

I sighed. It was Robert Ray, of course.

"You're early," I told him. "About two hours early."

"Andrew and I are going to dig for treasure," he said.

I took a breath. And then I smiled. "Nice," I said.

I took a caterpillar off the picnic table and put it gently in the grass.

Then my mother was outside with paper cups and plates and . . .

"I'm proud of you, Rosie," she said.

I didn't ask why. I knew why.

I was filled with the syrup of happiness again. And by the time everyone was coming up the path, I was ready.

Amy had skinned my hair back like Miss Deirdre's, except that Miss Deirdre had a red bow, and I had green.

Stephanie brought her wand, Karen her *Cinderella* outfit, and Miss Serena brought a box of candy.

Grandpa sat at the head of the table, of course.

Miss Deirdre held up her hand.

"Ta-ta-dum," said Miss Serena. She wiggled

her fingers as if she were playing the piano.

"This is not a performance of *Cinderella,*" Karen said.

"It's a rehearsal," said Stephanie.

Then we talked our way through *Cinderella* for Grandpa. Miss Serena *tum-de-tummed* on her make-believe piano.

Stephanie did some steps with her wand.

Karen held up her costume.

And I *pirouetted* around the patio . . . a wicked stepsister with a terrible frown.

Grandpa loved it.

At the last minute, I took a chance and did an *entrechat.*

I almost made it.

Just then Andrew came around the side of the house. He had cake on his face, mud on his hands, and . . . something else.

My mother looked up. "My earring," she said.

"Treasure," said Andrew.

Robert Ray was nodding.

I smiled at Robert, and at Andrew, and at Murphy, and at Grandpa.

I thought about the calendar upstairs. A month without Grandpa. I could do it.

I began another *entrechat.* This time, it was just right.

From Rosie's Notebook

Arabesque (Ar-e-BESK) Stand on one leg. Extend the other one to the back.

Barre (BAR) It's a handrail in front of a mirror. Hold on and warm up!

Battement tendu (Baht-MA ton-DUE) Heel up, slide one foot out, then back. Pretend you have a penny under your toes and you want to keep it on the floor.

Grand battement (GRON baht-MA) A great kick. I haven't learned this yet, but Genevieve does it in the picture. One leg is thrown up in the air. It looks great!

Bourée (Boo-RAY) Tiny traveling steps.

Choreography (Kor-ee-OG-ra-fee) The steps that are made up for a dance.

Entrechat quatre (on-truh-sha COT) Jump with one foot in front. Change your feet over, then change them back again before you land.

Jeté (zheh-TAY) A jump from one leg to the other.

Grand jeté (GRON zheh-TAY) A leap! One leg is stretched forward, and one leg back. This one looks super.

Piroutte (pir-oo-ET) Turn on one leg. Keep your other foot in back of your knee as you turn.

Plié (plee-AY) Bend with your knees out and your back

straight. Look in the mirror. See the diamond shape you've made. Then straighten back up.

Demi-plié (DEM-ee-plee-AY) A half knee-bend.

Relevé (reh-le-VAY) Rise to the balls of your feet. Keep your toes on the floor. Press down hard. (It's tiptoes.)